To my Grandd[...]
Aerianna

SCHOOL BUS CHATTER

THE THINGS WE HEAR FROM POINT A TO POINT B

Ellie Newsome

authorHOUSE

AuthorHouse™
1663 Liberty Drive
Bloomington, IN 47403
www.authorhouse.com
Phone: 1 (800) 839-8640

© 2015 Ellie Newsome. All rights reserved.

No part of this book may be reproduced, stored in a retrieval system, or transmitted by any means without the written permission of the author.

Published by AuthorHouse   11/09/2015

ISBN: 978-1-5049-5371-9 (sc)
ISBN: 978-1-5049-5372-6 (e)

Library of Congress Control Number: 2015916212

Print information available on the last page.

Any people depicted in stock imagery provided by Thinkstock are models, and such images are being used for illustrative purposes only.
Certain stock imagery © Thinkstock.

This book is printed on acid-free paper.

Because of the dynamic nature of the Internet, any web addresses or links contained in this book may have changed since publication and may no longer be valid. The views expressed in this work are solely those of the author and do not necessarily reflect the views of the publisher, and the publisher hereby disclaims any responsibility for them.

PREFACE

I love my job! I love kids! And I love to listen to them chatter. God has blessed me beyond measure with a job that I love! I give Him all the honor for also giving me the gift of laughter!

Two weeks ago I received my 20 year Safe Driving award from Cecil County Public Schools.
That means I have been doing a job I love for 20 years! I am now driving children who are the offspring of my former children! Most of the time, they love it when I tell them I know their parents. The things that kids tell me make me laugh. After about 3 years I decided I should really write these things down and eventually write a book so that you too might enjoy them and maybe even laugh a little.

I hope that when you read this you will imagine the tiny voice of a child saying the things that I have recorded.

Ellie Newsome

A great big thank you to the illustrator, Ms. Taylor Wyatt, who was a rider on my bus for Pre-Kindergarten, Kindergarten and her Senior year of high school.
And to Ms. Taylor Price for the front cover illustration.

Pre-Kindergarten

GIRL: "Miss Ellie, when I say 'Sugga Momma' that means you, OK?"
MRS ELLIE: "OK."
GIRL: "Sugga Momma"
MRS. ELLIE: "What?"
GIRL: "I love you."
MRS ELLIE: "I love you, too, 'Sugga Baby.'

⧖

"Don't the number 'free' sound like freeze?"

⧖

"In our heads, we have a brain." "In our body, we got bones, guts and 'bwood'."

⧖

"If someone ate my skin, I would be bones."
"What?"
"If someone ate my skin, I would be bones and eyes."

Ellie Newsome

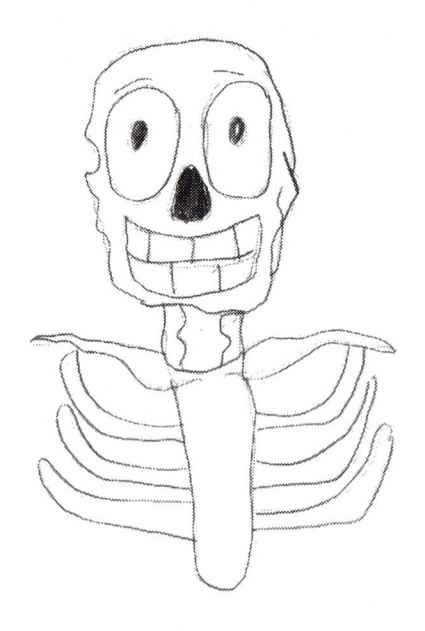

"Guess what I did to Timmy?"
"I fell in love with him."

"Guess what this boy did at our school?"
"He sat in bird poo-poo."

"Guess what I saw on the news?" "A bus 'falled' on a house."

"I like Friday cause it sounds like french fry."

"Sometimes I can touch my eyeball and it doesn't even hurt. Sometimes it makes me mad!"

∾

"I didn't mean to swallow the penny, I was just trying to hide it!"

∾

Boy: "A dog licks his butt, then licks me."
Me: "Don't say that. That's nasty."
Boy: That's actually what they do."

∾

I said, "Don't spit, it's nasty!" The little girl replied, "But, if we think we have a bug in our mouth, we have to spit out puke, so we don't get more sick."

∾

"You are one smart cookie,".
"I'm not a cookie."
"You're not?"
"No, I'm a pill."

∾

I picked up a dead bird and then I washed my hands, cause it can give you "weasels". "Weasels are chicken pops, right?"

Ellie Newsome

"I ate a bug. It was dried up."
"Ooh, that's gross!"
"That means I'm a meat eater. Is that right?"

༄

"I about puked. I was eating the crumbs out of my pocket and there was something black in it. It was a bug, I had put in my pocket!"

༄

"Sometimes I get to bounce on my Daddy's chubby belly."

༄

"My mommy is gonna buy me a fishing stick. It's gonna be a Barbie one and I'm gonna catch a big fish and we will eat it."

༄

"When people talk loud it makes me cough and choke." Someone said, 'Oh my gracious, you got a cold.'"

༄

"You won't see Chuckee the Mouse cause every time I go to McDonald's I don't see Ronald Donald."

༄

"Why do I smell my dad on this bus?"

"I'm really, really, really hot, cause I'm five now!"

∞

"A, B, C, D, E. F, G, W, X, Y, Z. Now I said my ABC's next time won't you sing with me?"

∞

Boy: "I'm going to the theater tonight."
Me: "What are ya gonna see, "Jack and the Beanstalk?"
Boy: "No, Pennsylvania. I have a date too."
In reality he is going to the school auditorium to see "Hotel Transylvania."

∞

"I have a brain. That's why I know stuff. If you play video games over and over and over you will have brain surgery."

∞

Pre-K Boy: "When I get home I'm gonna stab myself with a fork!"
Me: "Why would you do that?
Pre-K Boy:: "I'm gonna kill myself before Bigfoot does!"
His third grade cousin, very nonchalantly says, "Don't worry about it. His mom won't let him."

∞

Pre-K: "Lucky and lucky rhyme."
1st grader: "Lucky and lucky are the same word!"
Pre-K: "Oh."

Ellie Newsome

Me: "Child if you don't sit, I'm gonna have to talk to the principal."
Uninvolved Pre- K Boy: "Mrs. Ellie I thought you said 'pretzel butt' then I knew you said 'principal'!"

֍

Boy: "knock, knock"
Me: "who's there?"
Boy: "Head"
Me: "Head who?"
Boy: "My stop!"

֍

"I'm putting my brain in my mind."

֍

"When I get it a puppy, it's gonna be a boy and I'm gonna name him Seatbelter."

֍

When a little boy was whining about something,
I said "Aw, you poor thing."
He said, "I'm not a thing, I'm a kid!"
"And I'm not poor cause I'm not pouring!"

֍

"I'm almost 4, cause I'm 5."

֍

"When I grow up I'm gonna move far, far away and never brush my teeth again! That would be a ball!!"

KINDERGARTEN

"At outside today, I found a rock."

∽

"Stink bugs have a mind of their own!"

∽

"I can run faster than my sister. She is a medium."
(youngest sister of three)

∽

While staring out the window the little boy said, "sometimes I look at the bottom of the grass."

∽

"My cat Frankie, he died. My Dad threw him under the dirt and I put sticks on him. He likes sticks."

Ellie Newsome

After Sept. 11, 2001…..
"Something happened to our country. The men that were driving the planes at the buildings were mean men. They are still looking for people."

༄

"I have chocolate all on my face."
"Wanna know why?"
"Cause I have lots of cousins."

༄

"Oh, my head is freezing!".
"No, I mean it's hurting…Know why?.
Cause I hurt my knee last night."

THE IMPORTANT STUFF
"When we grow up, we can do anything we wanna do."
"And what are you gonna do?"
He answered, with a great big smile,
"Buy candy!"

༄

"Me missed the bus yesterday cause me Mommy had to go pee."

When I asked the Kindergarteners if any of them were allergic to red dye, one replied. "I'm allergic to water. That's why I don't want to get baptized."

"My bracelet is broken. I can't find it. It went to Heaven, I think."

"On Friday's they have mussels at Golden Corral. I ate about 10. I hate 'em but I still eat 'em."

"My grandma is in Florida cause she hates the cold. I think the cold gives her diahhrea."

"My Mommy's van is getting fixed. The beltloop and the water broke."

Ellie Newsome

"Yeah, we love Brittany Spears even though she's trashy."

※

"Mrs. Ellie, I have the wrong jacket on." I replied, "You do?" And she said, "There is another girl in my class that has a jacket just like mine. It is pink, just like mine and it has a Barbie on it, just like mine --- But, mine doesn't smell like fabric softener."

※

"Oh look, they've still got snow in their yard and we don't! How embarrassing!"

※

"Now that I'm five, I'm the goodest singer. I wanna be on the country singer. Please Lord, let me."

※

"I ride bus 219. Two, zero, nine, or should I say two, one, nine?"

※

"My new football can go in all kinds of weather except mud. It can go in land and rain but not dark."

School Bus Chatter

"Don't throw any body or anything from the bus."

❧

"All the windows are down! This is the greatest day of my life!!"

❧

"When someone is bad on the bus, maybe they need to be steparated to another bus."

❧

After she gave me flowers, the little girl asked, "Mrs. Ellie do you know why I gave you flowers? Cause I think I'm falling in love with you."

❧

As Fall approached, the Kindergarten class planned a trip to the local apple orchard. One of them, called it the "Apple Torture" and another said it was the "Apple Portrait."

❧

THE POWER OF THE MEDIA:

"Sunny D is the power of the Hulk" I saw it on TV."

Ellie Newsome

"There was a girl ghost named Mony Martel in the flooded bathroom."

∽

"I cried when we had a fire drill. I was scared of fire drills. I'm not anymore, I just shiver like I'm nervous."

∽

"I have the power to close my eyes and see through my mind."

∽

"Why does my teacher always wear those pretty clothes? Not like you, Mrs. Ellie."

∽

"Why don't you wear make-up, cause you're an old lady?"

∽

I hate dead creatures. They spit out blood and it gives me the creeps!"

∽

"I only like sloppy joe cause of the meat."

School Bus Chatter

"My hair sticks up like this cause Mommy puts glue on it."

∾

"My Mom can fix my bookbag cause she's magic. Well, my mom's a wizard and me and my sister are gonna be wizards too."

∾

"We missed the bus cause we were too much playing with our new Transformers."

∾

"I have a dad. He is old. He has some white in his beard. I think he has been on this world 6 years!"

∾

"I'm not dumber than a bag of peanuts!"

∾

"Oh man, I just swallowed my 'frow up'. I had a hair in my mouth and I had to 'frow' it up."

∾

"Saying 'Be careful' is another way of saying, 'I love you'"

Ellie Newsome

"When my Mom wrecked on the ice, she was doing donuts and then she put her tire on the tree and flipped her car over."

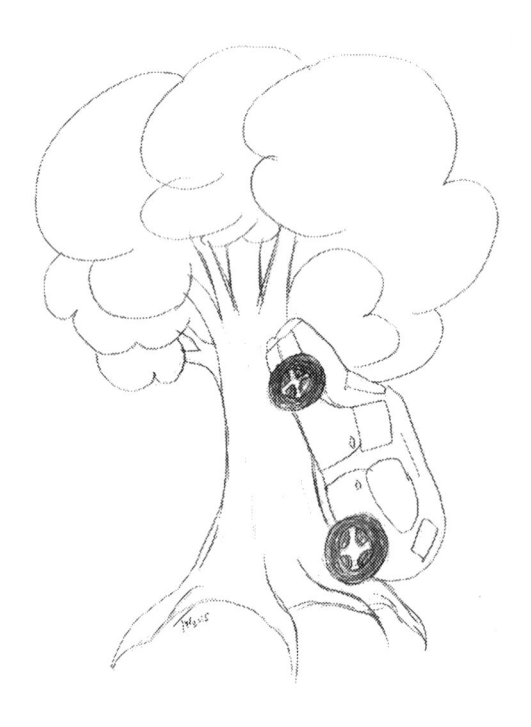

"It's Justin Beiber not Justin Beaver. If you call him Justin Beaver then it would sound like he is a beaver named Justin."

∞

"Wednesday is my relaxing day. That's why I don't like much people making noise."

School Bus Chatter

"One time a guy tooted so bad that my mom's real dad threw up!"

∾

"A certain amount of money equals a lot of money!"

∾

"When you grow up and the tooth fairy still has your teeth, she gives them back."

∾

"He accidently hit me with his ship and I am bleeding a triangle."

∾

"Do you know that in America some cops don't let you read Bible stories about God?"

∾

"I have two dads. One's fake and one's real."

∾

"I sleep in my toy box."

∾

"My cousin died."
"I'm sorry. How did he die?"
"He connected suicide."

Ellie Newsome

"Ouch! That hurt! Me and the window bumped heads!"

∽

"Last night I dreamed about a shed. I was in it for 3 days. God, Jesus and Mary took care of me. I said, 'God, I love you'."

∽

Boy: "Wow. There's a lot of kids in here!"
Girl: "It looks like three hundred million!"

∽

Girl: "I can't get that song out of my head."
Boy: "You better get it out or you are gonna break your brain!"

∽

"Let's pretend we have pancake breath."

∽

"I'm gonna have candy in class today! Real-live candy!!!

∽

"I bring Chapstick to school to keep my lips warm."

∽

ME: "You are one silly bird."
BOY: No, I am an angry bird!"

School Bus Chatter

"The sun is the boyfriend to the moon."

∾

"I stayed home yesterday. I had diarrhea in my underwear."

∾

"My nose was bleeding yesterday cause I was doing my homework."

∾

"A square is something that holds your roof up in the air."

∾

"When I am 6 I will get to sit in the thirst grade seat."

∾

"I heard someone say that bad word at school. I took it out of their brain and put it in mine."

∾

"My brother is starting to have a mustache."

∾

"I was so cold my oxygen froze!"

∾

"Chocolate's my life! I love chocolate! Without chocolate, I will die!"

Ellie Newsome

In a tiny little 5 year old voice, he said, "I try to control my anger but I can't. Every time I try to walk away from it, it just pulls me back in!"

∾

"It's very hard to control a bug's body. But I can control a bumble bee after I bonk it on the head."

∾

"Mrs. Ellie did you know parents have eyes in the back of their head? That's what my mom told me."

First Grade

"Monday is Show & Tell. I'm gonna tell them everything I know about this fake cricket."

∞

"Wanna know what kinda witch my mommy is? She's a vampire. But she's a good one!"

∞

"Last year my Kindergarten teacher was mean like the principal. Like she was the boss of the world! Guess what I got for my birthday? Deodorant."

∞

"I lost my tooth at school today but I don't think I will get any money cause it isn't very shiny and it smells bad."

Ellie Newsome

After getting money for losing another tooth,
He said... "I'm gonna be rich by the time I get done with these teeth!"

⌘

"Three French Hands, Two turtledoves."

⌘

"I'm very humiliated cause my dog is chasing the bus."

While waiting to unload at the elementary school two first grade girls had this discussion:
A: "Poppop and Mommom have a car like that, but they don't have a daughter or son anymore."
M: "Did they pass away?"
A: "No, they just growed up."

⌘

"When my Mom is mad at me she says all three of my names. She is loud. Really loud like a whale!"

"I wish the school had bus doors so you could drive us inside to drop us off."

∞

NOT YOUR TYPICAL "GIRL" COMMENT:
"Look how many geese there are and I'm not old enough to hunt!"

∞

"I forgot my lunchbox. I'm clumsy."

∞

"I'm gonna stay up early tonight!"

∞

"My mom is young, she just looks old. She is 22."

∞

"We saw a singing group last week and we saw their kids. The kids weren't real in person, they were just on paper."

∞

"When you go to 1st grade to separate classes your friendship is gonna be ripped apart!"

∞

"My mom has thirteen cavities."

Ellie Newsome

First grade girl:: "It smells like candy on this bus."
Kindergartener: "Probably my shoes."

〜

Oh, the compassion of a son: "For Halloween, be a clown and come to my house. My Mom's scared of clowns!"

"I'm actually eating something in my belly cause I'm starving. I'm eating my heart. No, I'm eating basghetti."

〜

"Sometimes my teacher sits on my desk and I sit in my chair. When she stands up, I touch the spot where she sat."
"Why?" I asked.
"I don't know." He replied.

School Bus Chatter

"My grandmom and granddad's holiday is me coming over to visit."

❦

"I made a behavior chart for my friend and every time she be's good I give her a prize."

❦

"I only writed Valentine's to my best friends and I writed, "here best friends" on them".

❦

Brother:"My mom threw up!"
Me: "Oh my! Is she sick?"
Sister: "It was cause of my snot!"
Brother: Yeah, she vomited!

❦

BROTHER: "I had a dream that our dog was dumb."
SISTER: "Oh no! That wasn't a dream! Our dog is stupid!"

Ellie Newsome

"My lizard did number one and number two on my hand, so really I should say he did number three!

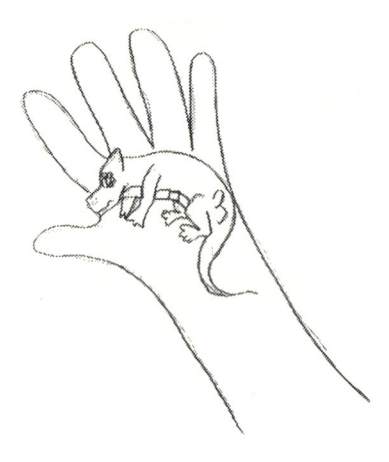

First Grade Boy: "Mrs. Ellie. Am I cool?"
Me: "What does cool mean?"
First Grade Boy: "Cool is doing popular things. My sisters don't think I'm cool."

∞

With his hair gelled and spiked just right, he asked me if he looked good and if I liked his ring. I said, "yeah". He said "I'm trying to look good for my girlfriend."

∞

"Yuck, I just burped up cauliflower!"

School Bus Chatter

"I made a rhyme. Six tricks in a tick.
Nine fell off. How many were left?"

~~~

"Last night I had to do homework. It was first grade and it was so hard I almost threwed up. Then I did throw up on the paper and they gave me another one and I threwed up and they sent me to the office."

~~~

"I'm so hungry I'm dreaming my friend is a pancake."

SECOND GRADE

As a going away present, I give my fifth graders a soda on the last day of school. A second grader said, "I hope they let you live till I get in 5th grade so I can get a soda."

∞

"Guess what, my mommy don't have no teeth!"

∞

After one child called another an idiot, I told them to use nice words, another girl said, "Yeah, fathers say those words when they fight."

∞

"Nobody should be disgruntled when bad things happen to them. One day my dad got hit when they were folding the cafeteria tables, and he got disgruntled."

Ellie Newsome

"State Troopers are more important than just police. They get to arrest people and stuff."

⋙

"I could never drive a bus. It would make me obnoxious!"

⋙

BOY: "When I grow up I want to work for the government".
ME: "Why would you want to do that?"
BOY: "So I can live on a farm."

Third Grade

Discussing the cow across the road. "She always lays down. She thinks she has a baby in her belly, but it already hatched!"

∞

"My Dad might have to go to the war. I hope he doesn't have to go. He is the only Dad I have. He works for the US Army National Guard."

∞

BEST EXCUSE EVER GIVEN FOR NOT PLAYING WITH A NEIGHBOR AFTER SCHOOL.
A 3rd grade boy talking to a Kindergarten girl, "I can't play because I have to watch my house…. I'm not kidding, it might float away. There is a pipe by the house that keeps bubbling. If it gets too bad, I have to stop it with my hand."
THE FUNNY THING IS…I think he really believed what he was saying.

"I don't want to get rain on a field trip. Your lunch will get soggy and I don't want a soggy lunch."

⌘

At 2:05 PM, he said "Good morning." instead of good afternoon. Then he said, "I got confused cause they both start with G"

⌘

"I know how to make snow. Put white cheese in a wood chipper. It works! It really does!!!"

⌘

"I didn't want to smell stinky, so I took a shower this morning."

⌘

"When I went to see Snow White and the guy said there were no words, just ballet, my eyeballs just about fell out of the balcony!"

School Bus Chatter

While doing a school project, A third grader learned that shark eggs are 'always fertilized'. He said, "I don't even know what 'always fertilized' means. Then he asked me to explain. I told him to ask his mom!

"Did you see me not acting like me?"

∞

"You wouldn't like it. Getting buried in the sand. It's worse than a tetnus shot."

∞

"Mrs. Ellie, I've got a 'bug' to pick with you!"

∞

"No one goes to the moon on a school day!"

Ellie Newsome

"Why did the robot cross the road? Cause it wanted to jump on the tractor. Does that make sense?"

༄

"I tried to stop school by throwing snowballs in the road."

༄

"Do you have to know how to drive to be a bus driver?"
I replied, "yes".
"That's what I thought."

༄

Our neighbor's rooster "cock-a-doodle-doos' 24-7!

Fifth Grade

A fifth grader was talking about the day they had a substitute driver.
"Use the directions! Not just the addresses. Every kid wants to get home ya know! It's liking fishing off the pier at Ocean City, you don't catch any fish! Fish are dumb in the summer"

∞

"We had kind of a rough morning cause our dog is having her period."

∞

On St. Patrick's Day one boy said "I am Irish, I'm just not feeling into green today."
I said, "Wow, I didn't know 5th grade boys cared about color."
His reply, "Unlike other 5th grade boys, I do have a sense of style."

Ellie Newsome

"Lottery just takes away your money. At poker at least you can win something. I won $50 last night."

∞

"If I could, I would take my Xbox and just hook it up in the bathroom. Wouldn't that be awesome?"

Ninth Grade

"Mrs. Ellie, is there a prohibition against electronical devices?"

༻༺

To a 9th grade boy, I said, "I know you have some family in West Virginia."
He said, "yeah, I like going to WV. We got some nice looking cousins!!!!!."

༻༺

"My belly button is itching."

༻༺

I gave up meat for Ash Wednesday but I only lasted 3 days."

Ellie Newsome

"Tomorrow we're not cooking. We're watching a video about pancakes."

☻

"We're gonna decorate the tree tonight, you know all the utensils, ornaments and stuff.

Tenth Grade

"The worst life to live would have to be the life of a frog. They have such a sticky tongue if they eat a bug that tastes awful – they can't even spit it out."

Ellie Newsome

When I asked him how far along his Mom was in her pregnancy, He said, "She's just now starting to wear fraternity clothes."

When his sister walked by without responding to his hello, he asked, "Whatsa matter? Cat just bite your ear?"

BEST EVER MADE-UP WORD: disruptful

"I can't get in trouble on the bus because then I would have no way to get to school to get in trouble there."

Eleventh Grade

WELL SAID….
11th grader: "You love me."
Me: "I know, cause God says I have to."
11th grader: "You must do it with a willing heart, or it doesn't count."

༄

First 11th grade guy: "She's always worrying what people think about her."
Second 11th grade guy: "When 99% of the time no one is even thinking about her!"

༄

"Mrs. Ellie, I am so bored, I'm getting on my own nerves!"

Ellie Newsome

"There ought to be a law against going to school when the sun is so bright that the passengers can't see where they're going."

∞

After an 11th grade was boy was mildly belligerent the day before, he brought me a long-stemmed rose the next day. No words "I'm sorry" but I knew what he meant. ☺

TWELFTH GRADE

While discussing how "old" people always read the obituaries, a 2010 senior said, "reading the obituaries just bring you down and isn't it funny how they always die in alphabetical order."

Ellie Newsome

RANDOM ADDITIONS

FIRST DAY OF SCHOOL 2009/2010

I picked up two sisters early in my route because they were already out when I went by their house.

I'm glad I did. By the time I got to the intersection in Pilotown I noticed a very large grasshopper on my sun visor. I wasn't really wanting to touch it. Sister One said she would get it. I stopped the bus and she came up and touched it. It jumped, she squealed! Sister Two tried next. She took hold of its antenna and pulled but the little sticky feet held firm. So she took her sneaker off and coerced the bug into her shoe. Then she stood at the steps and shook her shoe outside. When she returned to her seat, she put her hand in the shoe to make sure it was empty. It was. We had gone about 1/10 of a mile when Sister One said "Hey Sister, that grasshopper is on your back!" So I had to stop again, the girls got off the bus and Sister One was finally able to swish her hand hard enough to get the bug off Sister Two and we proceeded to school! What a great first morning!

∞

I took three teachers on a field trip. At the drop off, they got off together.

Teacher 1: "You are bus 400?"

Me: "No. 20"

Teacher 3: "Are you 400 or 40?"

Me: "20"

Should they really be teaching? The number is on my bus in five different places!!

School Bus Chatter

The kid's favorite Winter song, written by me
(tune of Jingle Bells)
"Dashing thru the snow, in a great big yellow bus
It's to school we go, now don't you make a fuss
It's where you learn and play, we go there every day
Dashing thru the snow in a great big yellow bus.
Oh!!! yellow bus, yellow bus dashing thru the snow
Up the hills and around the curves
It's to school we go!"

∽∽

And finally,

"I wish the world was full of butterflies and ladybugs."

Printed in the United States
By Bookmasters